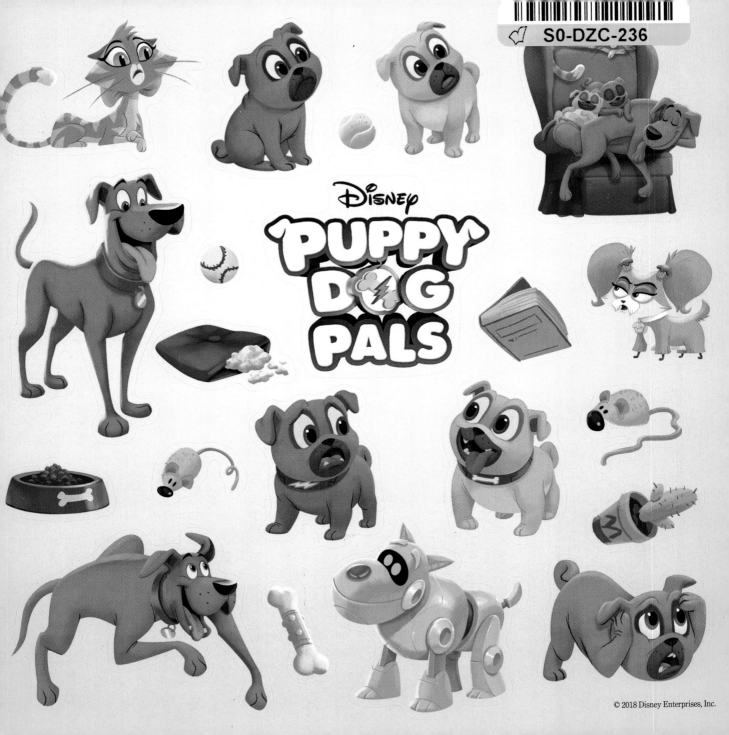

Adventures in Puppy-Sitting

ADAPTED BY **ANNIE AUERBACH**

BASED ON THE EPISODE WRITTEN BY **JESSICA CARLETON**

FOR THE SERIES CREATED BY **HARLAND WILLIAMS**

ILLUSTRATED BY THE **DISNEY STORYBOOK ART TEAM**

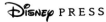

Los Angeles · New York

SUSTAINABLE
FORESTRY
INITIATIVE

Certified Sourcing

www.sfiprogram.org
SFI-01415

One morning, Bob wakes up Bingo and Rolly with some good news.

"Morning, sleepy-snouts!" he says. "Guess what, guys? My friend got a new puppy named Baby."

Baby? Bingo and Rolly think that's a funny name for a puppy.
"She doesn't want the puppy to get lonely while she's at work,"
Bob says, "so I said Baby can stay here with you today, and you can
keep her company!"

The puppies think this is a *great* idea!

As soon as Bob leaves to get Baby, Bingo turns to Rolly.
"Let's get ready!" Their mission is to be the best puppy-sitters ever!
"Great puppy-sitters always have food ready," says Bingo.
Rolly agrees. "So let's give Baby her own dish to make her feel at home!"

Bingo finds a small teacup to use as
Baby's bowl. "If we each share a few of our
kibbles, that'll fill it up," he explains.
"Bow and wow!" says Rolly.

"What else do great puppy-sitters do?" Rolly asks.

"They're good at making sure puppies get naps," Bingo says.

"Baby could sleep in one of Bob's shoes. That's what you two goofballs used to do," Hissy reminds the pups.

Bingo and Rolly remember sleeping in "Loafy," Bob's old loafer shoe, and go searching for it.

In Bob's closet, the puppies burrow through a pile of Bob's shoes. Rolly pulls out the oldest, rattiest one. "Loafy!" he yells. "My old sleeping shoe! And I still fit. . . . Sort of . . . Not really."

The pups are sure that little Baby will love sleeping in **Loafy**!

Next Bingo and Rolly wonder what kinds of toys little puppies play with.

"Okay, first of all, *you're* still puppies," Hissy tells them.

"We mean when we were even *littler* puppies," Rolly says.

Hissy shows them a photo. "Well, you loved this squeaky toy. I used to throw it for you to fetch when I was bored."

Bingo's eyes get wide. "You mean Mr. Mousey?" he asks. "I haven't seen that squeaky toy in forever!"

Bingo and Rolly run to find Mr. Mousey. He's old and worn and his nose is falling off. But the puppies know Baby will still love him!

Just then, Bingo and Rolly hear the front door open. Bob is home with the puppy! They run over, excited to meet little Baby.

"Come on in, Baby. It's okay," Bob reassures her.

When the new puppy walks through the door, Hissy and the pups are in for a great big surprise. Little Baby is a gigantic Great Dane puppy!

"Whoa. That is one big baby," Bingo says, looking up—way, way up—at the new arrival.

Hissy quickly stands up and then hightails it out of the room. "Good luck with the puppy-sitting," she calls. "If you need me, I'll be hiding . . . I mean, napping."

Rolly just shakes his head. "She is *not* going to fit in that shoe."

After Bob leaves for work, Baby starts whimpering and crying.

"Don't worry, Baby," Rolly says. "It's our mission to be the greatest puppy-sitters ever!"

Bingo nudges Mr. Mousey toward her. Baby sniffs the toy, gives it a quick lick, and in three seconds flat, she's off!

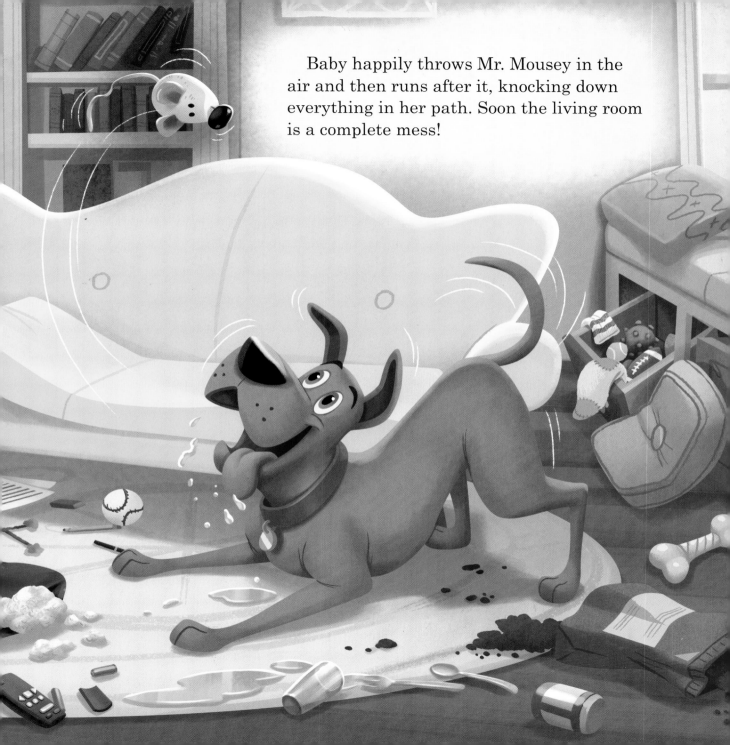

Baby happily throws Mr. Mousey in the
air and then runs after it, knocking down
everything in her path. Soon the living room
is a complete mess!

The puppies realize they have to find something else for Baby to do before the living room gets completely ruined. "I know what *I* always want to do," says Rolly. "Eat!"

The pups lead Baby into the kitchen and offer her the small teacup of food they had prepared. But Baby devours her food in one bite . . . and then eats both bowls of Bingo and Rolly's food, too!

After her meal, Baby tosses Mr. Mousey onto the kitchen table. Then she jumps up to fetch it and tips the table over, sending everything on it crashing to the ground!

"We'd better get Baby outside before she destroys the house!" Bingo says.

As the three pups go outside, A.R.F. zooms in to do what he does best: clean up!

In the backyard, Rolly and Bingo decide to teach Baby some tricks.

Bingo shows Baby how to sit. "Sit on your bottom, like this," he says.

Baby copies Bingo and sits down. Unfortunately, she sits right on Rolly!

"Now let's teach her to stand up," Rolly groans.

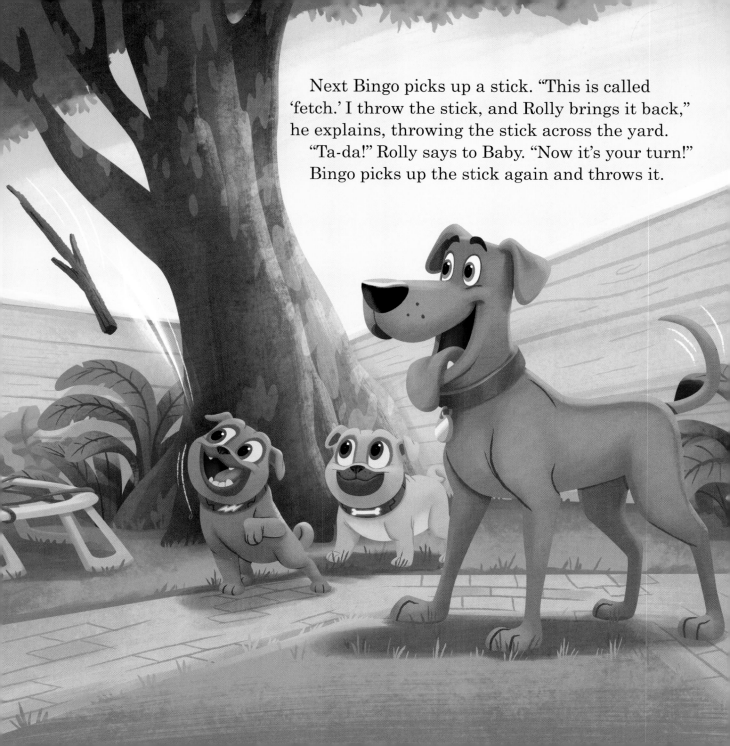

Next Bingo picks up a stick. "This is called 'fetch.' I throw the stick, and Rolly brings it back," he explains, throwing the stick across the yard.

"Ta-da!" Rolly says to Baby. "Now it's your turn!" Bingo picks up the stick again and throws it.

But instead of fetching the stick, Baby comes back with an entire tree in her mouth!

Rolly shakes his head. "If we stay here, Baby might destroy the whole yard!"

"I know!" Bingo says. "Really great puppy-sitters would take a puppy to the dog park. Let's go!"

After Bingo, Rolly, and Baby leave for the park, A.R.F. looks around at the extra big mess. He can't wait to clean it up!

At the dog park, Baby runs around excitedly as Bingo and Rolly show her all the neat stuff there is to do there.

"Baby sure seems happy!" Bingo says, watching Baby explore.

"Look at us being great puppy-sitters!" Rolly exclaims.

Suddenly, the pups see a stick flying through the air.
Bingo and Rolly take off after it!
Baby starts to follow them, but then she hears a SQUEAK!

Across the park, Baby spots a squeaky toy! Joyfully, she runs over and picks it up.

But the squeaky toy belongs to a dog named Cupcake.

"What's the big idea?" Cupcake snaps at Baby. "That's mine!"

Cupcake grabs the toy and pulls. Baby tugs back . . . until Cupcake narrows her eyes and growls.

Baby lets go.
"Go find your own squeaky toy!" Cupcake says.
Baby's eyes brighten, and then she
runs off without looking back.

Meanwhile, Bingo and Rolly bring the stick back to its owner. "Now *that's* how you play fetch, Baby!" Bingo says. He turns to find her, but she's gone! The puppies look all around the dog park, but Baby is nowhere to be found!

Cupcake walks over to them. "Are you looking for the big drooly puppy that tried to take my squeaky toy before she ran out of here?" she asks.

Rolly nods. "Which way did she go?"

Cupcake just shakes her head. "Only you two could lose the biggest puppy in the dog park."

"She *is* the biggest!" Bingo realizes. "Rolly, we just have to follow the biggest paw prints."

"Like this one?" Rolly asks, looking at a large paw print in the dirt.

"Exactly!" Bingo replies. He looks around and finds a whole trail of big paw prints. "Follow those paw prints! Thanks, Cupcake!"

"Aw, biscuits. I wasn't trying to help!" Cupcake calls after them.

Bingo and Rolly follow the paw prints out of the park and through the neighborhood until they realize they are headed straight for their house.

"I think I figured it out," Bingo says. "Baby was trying to play with Cupcake's squeaky toy right before she ran off."

"She's going back to our house for Mr. Mousey!" Rolly exclaims. "Let's go!"

Back at the house, the pups are delighted to find Hissy playing fetch with Baby and Mr. Mousey.

"High paw, Rolly!" says Bingo.

Rolly smiles at his brother. "High paw, Bingo!"

"I've got to admit, it's kind of fun to have a puppy around to play this game again," Hissy says.

"You know, we're still puppies, too," says Rolly.

Hissy shrugs. "Then get in this game. There's room for two more!"

Later, when Bob gets home, the house is quiet. He finds all the animals snuggled up together.

"Wow! The puppy really tuckered you all out, huh?" Bob says with a smile. Bingo and Rolly sleepily open their eyes. "Looks like you ended up being great puppy-sitters."

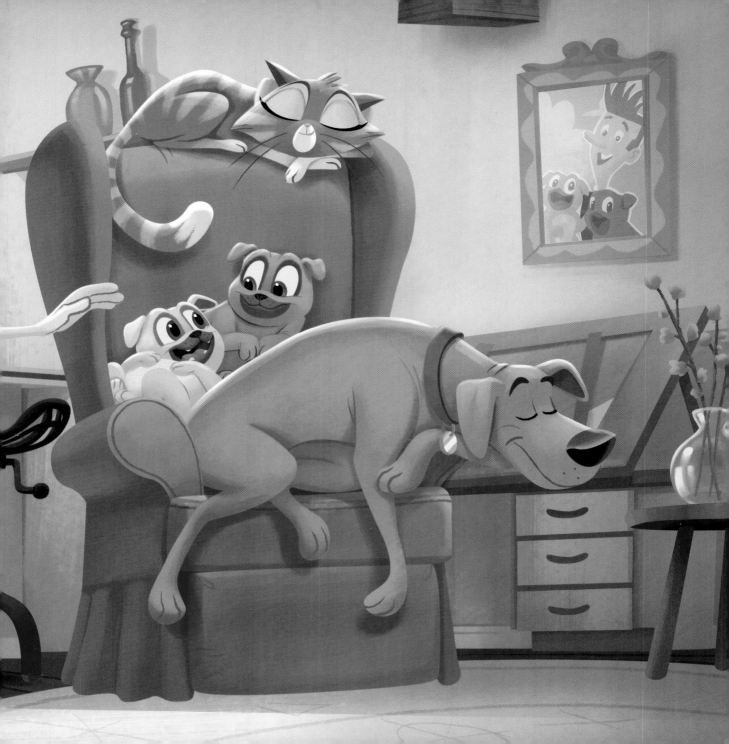

Yup! It's been a big day for the little puppy-sitters!

MISSION ACCOMPLISHED